NUMBEARS

NUMBEARS

A Counting Book

By Kathleen Hague

Illustrated by Michael Hague

SCHOLASTIC INC.

New York   Toronto   London   Auckland   Sydney

ISBN 0-590-46234-2

Text copyright © 1986 by Kathleen Hague.
Illustrations copyright © 1986 by Michael Hague.
All rights reserved. Published by Scholastic Inc.,
730 Broadway, New York, NY 10003,
by arrangement with Henry Holt and Company, Inc.

12 11 10 9 8 7 6 5 4 3   3 4 5 6 7/9

Printed in the U.S.A.   09

First Scholastic printing, February 1993

This book is dedicated to Mr. Rogers.
We like him just the way he is.

Michael and Kathleen Hague

Although there is no one else around,

Meghan's not one bit lonely;

She always has one special friend,

It's her—the one and only!

Sam says it's easy buttoning his coat,

But it's tricky tying his shoe;

He says when he's done, with a sigh of relief,

"I'm lucky I only have two."

Brittany wrote her good friends a note,

Inviting them both to tea;

Becky came and Page did too,

They're the best of friends these three.

Kathleen's seen a nest out her window,

Up high on the second floor;

Snug inside the basket of twigs

Are blue eggs—she counted four.

Mikey's built five jolly snowmen;

One has a scarf and a vest.

He's put a bow tie on another.

And snow hats on all of the rest.

Alison loves a day at the beach,

Collecting shells by the shore;

She found six and said, "That's enough,

Because I can't hold anymore."

Cori walked down to the park today,

With seven ducks all in a row;

Around the pond and up the street,

They'd follow wherever she'd go.

Elisa loves her eight little dolls;

She rocks each one on her lap,

Brushes their hair, serves them their lunch,

And sees that each one gets a nap.

Anthony watched the astronauts fly

Their spaceship up to the moon;

He tied nine balloons to his backyard craft,

And has scheduled the blast-off for noon.

Mary likes watching little clouds play,

Changing their shapes in the sky;

To her delight, she's just caught sight

Of ten fluffy lambs floating by.

Kevin has some unusual bunnies,

He winds each one with a key;

They form an eleven-piece band,

And play their concerts for free.

Heath has quite a collection of balls,

To throw, to kick, and to hit;

There are twelve of them scattered around his room,

So there's scarcely a place left to sit.

Whether counting themselves or their favorite toys,

These bears can count with great ease.

It doesn't matter how few or how many,

For they now know their one, two, threes.

Designer: Marc Cheshire
Production Editor: Victoria Mathews
Production Manager: Karen Gillis

Composition: Waldman Graphics, Inc., Pennsauken, New Jersey
Color Separations: Offset Separations Corporation, Turin, Italy